CHAKROL
THE OCEAN HAMMER

With special thanks to Michael Ford

For Tana Coulson

www.seaquestbooks.co.uk

ORCHARD BOOKS

First published in Great Britain in 2014 by Orchard Books
This edition published in 2016 by The Watts Publishing Group

3 5 7 9 10 8 6 4 2

Text © 2014 Beast Quest Limited.
Cover and inside illustrations by Artful Doodlers with special thanks to Bob and Justin
© Orchard Books 2014

Series created by Beast Quest Limited, London

A CIP catalogue record for this book is available from the British Library.

ISBN 978 1 40832 859 0

Printed in Great Britain

Orchard Books
An imprint of Hachette Children's Group
Part of The Watts Publishing Group Limited
Carmelite House, 50 Victoria Embankment, London EC4Y 0DZ

An Hachette UK Company
www.hachette.co.uk
www.hachettechildrens.co.uk

CHAKROL
THE OCEAN HAMMER

THE PRIDE OF BLACKHEART

BY ADAM BLADE

ORCHARD

GOLDEN ISLAND

THE COLD PEAKS

GRAVEYARD

AQUORA

SUMARA

UNDERTOW

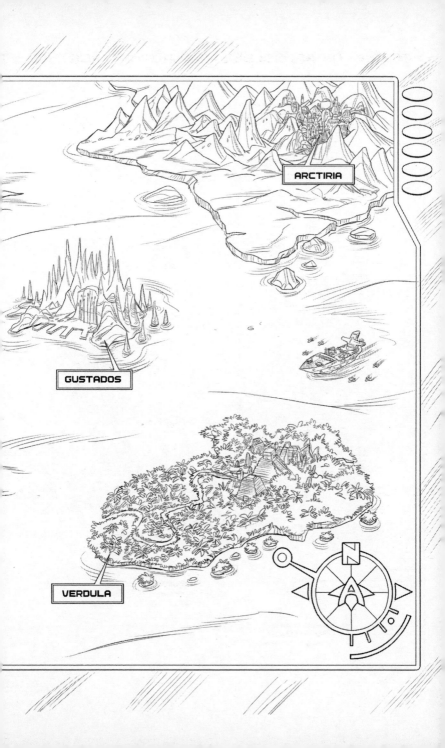

```
>FROM: CAPTAIN REAVER OF THE PRIDE
       OF DELTA
>TO:   THE DELTA QUADRANT ALLIANCE
```

URGENT – PLEASE RESPOND

Mayday! Hostile vessels were detected at 1632 hours off the starboard bow. The Pride of Delta has now been boarded by pirates. I am not sure how long we have...

Be aware, the Kraken's Eye will soon be in the hands of the pirates. Please do whatever is necessary to secure the keys. The pirates must not be allowed to operate the weapon.

Rest assured I will not surrender the ship. We will remain in position until we receive a response, or until the ship is taken by force...

END

Message delivered: 1648 hours – Responses: 0

CHAPTER ONE

AQUORA UNDER ATTACK

Max shot through the depths of the sea, holding on tight to the handlebars of his aquabike. Above the thrum of the engine, he felt his communicator headset vibrate.

"Come in, Max! It's Callum."

Max reached for the transmit button.

"I'm here, Dad. Have you found the *Pride of Blackheart*?" The last time Max had seen him, Callum had been sailing ahead with the Aquoran fleet, chasing Cora Blackheart and her gang of pirates.

"Yes, and it's just as we feared. She's heading right for Aquora," his dad replied. "But your uncle must have boosted the engines – we can't keep up!"

Max shot a glance at Lia, who was cutting through the water beside him on her pet swordfish, Spike. Next to her, their pirate friend Roger zoomed along, arms held tight to his side, propelled by his rocket boots. They'd recently left the island of Gustados, but were well on their way to Max's home city of Aquora now. Max, Lia and Roger had already left the Gustadian navy behind and were catching up with the Aquoran fleet by the second.

"It's up to us now," Max told Lia, shutting off his communicator. "We need to get to Aquora before the pirates!"

Lia nodded, her silver hair streaming in the water. She spoke in strange clicks to Spike and the swordfish shot off with a twitch of his tail. Roger twisted a dial on his wrist and disappeared after her.

"Race, Max?" Rivet barked.

Max grinned. "Better hang on, Riv," he said. The dogbot's metal paws clamped onto the aquabike, and Max twisted the throttle to full power.

The burst of speed almost pulled Max off the seat, but he crouched lower and clung on. They streaked beneath the shadows of massive ships above – the ships of Aquora. Max's dad was on board the Aquoran flagship, leading them in pursuit of Cora.

But the city is defenceless, thought Max, tightening his grip on the aquabike's handlebars. *And if we don't get there in time, it won't matter how many ships we have, because Cora Blackheart will invade it and take the key to activate the Kraken's Eye.*

The Kraken's Eye. Even the name made Max shudder. It was a weapon on board the *Pride of Blackheart*, powerful enough to destroy entire islands. Any one of four keys could operate the Kraken's Eye, and so far he and Lia had got hold of three, each one hidden in a different island city. The fourth was hidden in Aquora and they knew Cora would stop at nothing to get it. They might have stood a chance against her, but Cora had an accomplice: Max's cruel uncle, the Professor. In the ship's state-of-the-art lab he had created deadly Robobeasts, hybrids of robots and sea creatures, created with genetic engineering. The Robobeasts had no fear. No pity. They were designed only to kill.

And if I know my uncle, there'll be another getting ready to attack Aquora, Max thought.

Max barely noticed the underwater vista speeding past. He kept his eyes on the compass bearing, heading straight for the city he once called home. Not far now…

SLAM!

He twisted the handlebars as something smacked into the water above in a haze of bubbles. A chill settled over his heart as he saw it was the burned-out wreckage of an Aquoran defence boat. It sank slowly into the depths.

We're too late, he thought.

"Let's take a look," said Lia, pointing upwards.

Max lifted the bike's nose and climbed to the surface. As he broke out into fresh air, the first sounds he heard were the city's alarm sirens. Then he saw flames, and a bombardment of missiles flashing ahead. It had been ages since he'd seen his home city, and he gasped in horror at the sight that met his eyes.

The defence shield was raised – thick

titanium walls ringing the island and rising
three storeys high. Behind them stood the
gleaming skyscrapers of Aquora, like fragile
needles pointing into the sky. Cora's ship,
the *Pride of Blackheart*, floated in the outer
harbour, dwarfing every other vessel, her
battle-scarred hull painted with black skulls.
Cora had her biggest blaster cannons firing
at one point on the titanium barrier. More
blasters bristled from the ship's sides, keeping

the Aquoran subs and flying pods at bay.

As Max watched, another sub was blasted apart in a shower of molten metal.

The sooner his father and the main fleet arrived, the better.

"Scallywags!" said Roger. "Your crew ain't faring too well, are they?"

"We need to get on board the *Blackheart*," said Lia, appearing beside him on the surface. She was wearing her Amphibio mask so she could breathe above water. "If we can disable those guns, we might stand a chance."

Roger smiled behind the visor of his deep-suit. "Good plan, fish-girl," he said. "And once we get on board, we can find Max's ma." He gave Max a wink with his one good eye.

"If she's even there," said Max. Roger was sure that Cora must have Max's mum prisoner, since the Professor had created a clone of her to trick Max. But Max didn't feel so certain. He didn't want to get his hopes up again, only to have them crushed.

"Have faith, matey," said Roger.

"We've got to sneak up," said Max. "Not do anything rash… Roger, wait!"

The pirate was already shooting off towards the enormous battleship.

"He's going to get himself killed!" said Lia.

As Roger neared the scarred pirate ship, he waved his arms at it. "Hey-ho, me hearties.

I've got something for you!"

At least a dozen guns swivelled their barrels towards him.

"What's he *doing*?" said Lia.

Roger reached into his tunic. Max wondered if he was about to draw a blaster pistol. *If he does, he'll be dead before he pulls the trigger…*

"Roger not clever!" barked Rivet.

But it wasn't a weapon Roger pulled out. It was one of the keys to the Kraken's Eye – the one he'd stolen from the Gustadians.

"Roger, no!" said Max. "We have to stop him!"

The *Blackheart's* guns opened fire with a deafening roar. Roger dropped the key, rolled in the water and dived as the waves exploded around him. "Yikes! Ouch! Steady on!"

Max steered the aquabike through the flashes and spray, with Rivet still clinging on behind him. He could see two pirate attack subs already heading for Roger and the sinking key. One of them turned its guns on Lia and Spike.

"Noooo!" shouted Max.

SPLAT!

A ball of white gloop suddenly shot through the water and slammed into the nearest sub, coating its viewing shield. Almost at once it began to sink, pulled down by the weight of the strange substance. The second sub extended a robotic grabber to snatch the key from the water.

SPLAT!

Another blob snapped the grabber off and sent the sub spinning away.

Max turned and his heart leaped as he saw a Gustadian warship approaching. It looked like it was made of modelling clay, rippling in every colour of the rainbow. Its strange cannons were smoking from firing the gloop. Max signalled with a thumbs up. The Gustadians' attack had bought them valuable time.

Quickly he dived below the surface and scanned the underside of the *Pride of Blackheart*, looking for a way in. Lia swam up to him, the key in her hand. Max saw a wide hatch, halfway along the hull. *Weird*, he thought. *I'm sure I didn't see that last time I was on board the ship.* He pointed to it. "There!" he said to Lia.

"So my plan worked!" said Roger, arriving at their side.

Max rolled his eyes. "Er…what plan, exactly? To almost get yourself blasted into plankton?"

"To distract them!" said Roger.

Max rolled his eyes and jumped off the aquabike, drawing his hyperblade and swimming for the hatch with Lia and Roger at his side. He was just wondering how they'd get in when there was a deep whirring sound, and the hatch opened. His heart stopped.

Something was coming out. A monstrous grey body, packed with muscle, cut effortlessly through the water. Its head was wider than its body, with bulbous eyes at each side and

a wide, gaping mouth. *A hammerhead shark!* The Professor's additions were clear – its back was coated in sleek polished metal, making it look like an Aquoran battle cruiser. The Robobeast's eyes were glassy and black. As it opened its enormous mouth to reveal rows of vicious, pointed metal teeth, Max backed away in panic – his hyperblade felt about as useful as a toothpick.

We need to get out of here, Max realised. But before he could begin to think about how, two rocket launchers extended from the Robobeast's sides.

They swivelled, pointing right at Max.

CHAPTER TWO

CHAKROL

The rocket launchers flared as they fired. Max brought up his arm and twisted in the water. Two jet streams passed centimetres away on either side of him, and shot off into the empty water.

"Ha, you missed him!" shouted Roger.

Max saw two more rockets loading into the firing chambers.

It's not going to miss again.

"Max, ye scurvy dog!" cried Roger. "Get over here now!"

Max felt Roger grip his shoulder firmly and yank him through the water. The huge bulk of the Robobeast edged towards them in pursuit, but Roger's boots blasted a stream of bubbles and they shot out of range.

"Where are we going?" asked Max.

"There!" shouted Roger, pointing further along the bottom of the ship.

At first Max couldn't see anything apart from barnacles and rust, but then he spotted it. Another hatch. Tiny, barely large enough for a person to fit through.

"Look out!" yelled Lia, as a rocket shot past.

"Riv," said Max. "I need you to head to Callum's ship." He pressed a button on the dogbot's back, and Rivet's back compartment whirred open. Then he took the Gustadian key from Lia and stowed it inside Rivet, together with the Arctirian and Verdulan keys. *No sense in taking them on board.* They'd be much safer with Rivet.

"Leave, Max?" said the dogbot.

"Yes, boy, off you go!" said Max.

"You too," said Lia, patting Spike on the flank. "Be careful!"

The swordfish looked at Lia for a second, then shot off after Rivet. *I just hope the pair of them can look after those keys*, thought Max. Roger was setting to work prising open the circular hatch with his hook. Meanwhile the hammerhead monster was reloading again and looming closer. Max couldn't help thinking it was grinning.

"Some time today would be great, Roger," said Lia.

The pirate braced his feet against the hull and heaved. "Almost…there, mateys!"

The Robobeast brought its rockets level, its mouth gaping.

CRACK!

The hatch swung open and debris filled the water, gushing over them. Max picked out the smell of rotten food and engine oil. He saw scrap metal, vegetable peelings, bones and wiring. Through the cloud of rubbish, the Robobeast was rotating its rockets, trying to pick them out.

"It's a garbage chute," said Lia in disgust, clutching her nose.

"Beggars can't be choosers," Roger replied. "Get in there, sharpish!"

The pirate went first, heading into the hatch. Lia followed, grimly. Max cast a final look back at the Robobeast. It turned slowly in the water like a battleship changing direction. On its side he caught sight of an engraved metal plaque, reading *CHAKROL*.

Max tucked his hyperblade into his belt and gripped the side of the chute, heaving himself in. Something told him this wouldn't be the last time he had to face Chakrol.

The water was gloomy with filth, but soon Max's hands located the rungs of a ladder and he found himself climbing up into air. They must have passed through the waterline. Lia stood on the rungs above, attaching her Amphibio mask so she could breathe.

"Your uncle's Robobeasts get worse every time," she said.

"Tell me about it," said Max. He tweaked his communicator. "Dad? Come in!"

After a hiss, his headset crackled. "Max? It's Callum. Where are you?"

"I'm on Cora's ship. We almost got chomped by a giant hammerhead shark called Chakrol. I'm going to look for Mum."

"What do you mean?" asked his dad. "Your mum's gone, Max. Years ago."

Max felt his heart sink, and wished he'd never mentioned it. "It's a long story, Dad," he said. "But I have a theory that Mum's—"

A burst of sound exploded in Max's ear and he heard cries through the headset. Then the connection cut out.

"Dad!"

"Is everything all right?" asked Lia.

"I hope so," Max said quietly.

"Quit chattering, you two," said Roger, climbing off the ladder. "Where to now?"

Max followed Lia, picking what looked like a bit of potato peel off his shoulder. They found themselves above the chute, in a chamber filled with rubbish. "We need to find Cora and stop the pirates," said Lia.

"*After* we track down my mum," said Max, with steel in his voice. "I'm not leaving this ship without her."

Lia shook her head. "We can't do both, Max."

"Actually, perhaps we can," said Roger. "I know this ship like the back of my hand."

"How?" asked Max, narrowing his eyes.

Roger tapped the side of his nose with his hook. "Let's just say Cora and I go a long way back. Anyway, if I can scramble the power circuits, it might distract the pirates a bit. Lia can tackle them while you look for your ma. Once you've sprung her from the brig, we can team up and deal with this scurvy crew. What could go wrong?"

Max shared a glance with Lia that said, *Just about everything*, but he nodded anyway. They didn't have many options. "Let's do it."

Roger led them along a low corridor, lined with white ceiling lights. Max drew his hyperblade again, keeping his ears open for footsteps. If a pirate patrol stumbled across them now, it was over.

Soon Roger reached a panel on the wall and ripped it open, revealing circuit boards beneath. "Electrics were never my strong point, but this ought to do the trick." He jammed his hook into the wiring and pulled a clump of cables loose in a shower of sparks. Max winced. Everything went dark for a few seconds, then the emergency lights came on. Around the ship, Max heard the echo of crew members crying out in surprise. *They'll know they've got intruders now*, he thought. *We haven't got long.*

Roger pointed. "Follow this passage, take the third on the left, and head down two flights," he said. "You'll find the brig down there. Good luck."

Max headed off, guided only by the glowing red lights set every few paces along the corridor. In the back of his mind, he wondered how exactly Roger knew so much about the *Pride of Blackheart*. Their pirate friend had once sailed with Cora, but how close had the pair of them been? With every step, Max's heart beat harder in his chest. *If Roger's right, my mother's here somewhere. After all these years, I might only be seconds away from seeing her again...*

The main steel door to the brig was locked by a magnetic keypad. Max opened the control panel with trembling fingers and examined the wiring. *Not too complicated.* He twisted two wires across one another, bypassing the security. The door clunked open and the foul smell of unwashed bodies hit him. The narrow passage beyond was lined with cells on either side, still closed, thankfully. The ceiling lights flashed fitfully, throwing the corridor into sudden gloom before brightening again.

Max ran quickly along, throwing glances into each cell. He saw figures crouched or throwing themselves against the bars. Scrawny limbs; desperate starving faces.

"Let me out!" cried a voice.

"Don't leave us!" said another.

Max passed them at a jog. *She has to be here somewhere…*

Doubts crept into the back of Max's mind. What if she wasn't here at all? What if all his hopes were foolish daydreams and she'd died years before?

Max reached the final cell. A figure stood at the back, facing away. But from the long hair trailing down her back, he knew at once it was the person he was looking for.

His mother.

His stomach felt light and heavy at the same time. All the moisture seemed to leave

his mouth. His knees trembled and the voices
of the other prisoners died away.

"Mum!" he said. *I've found her. After all
these years…* It looked like the cell was locked
manually. Max put down his hyperblade
and drew back the bolts, yanking the sliding
door aside, heart thudding almost painfully.
"Mum, it's me, Max!" The lights failed again,

and all was dark. He stepped into the cell. "Mum?" he said, his doubts flooding back.

He saw her turn, just as the overhead lights flashed on. And what he saw brought a scream to his lips.

CHAPTER THREE

HUG OF DEATH

Her face had gone. Instead there was just a mess of wires and metal workings. One eyeball rotated on a stalk, and metal jaws gnashed over and over.

Max staggered backwards, his heart filling with relief and terror at the same time. *It's not her!* It was the clone again – the one he'd battled in the ice city of Arctiria. He'd last seen this thing falling from a cliff. It couldn't have survived.

But his eyes told him that it had.

It's a trap, Max realised. *My uncle and Cora knew that if I got on board, I'd come down here.*

"Hello, Max," said the clone, its voice half human, half robotic. "It's so good to see you again!"

It lunged at him, arms raking the air.

Max dodged sideways and the robot leaped

past him, slamming into the wall opposite and collapsing in a heap. With the sound of grinding metal, it pushed itself to its feet.

"Come to me, Max," it said. "Give your mother a hug."

Max saw his hyperblade at the thing's feet and decided not to risk lunging for it. He turned and ran back along the corridor. Looking over his shoulder, he saw the robot coming after him, dragging one foot along the floor. The clone still wore the red-panelled wetsuit he'd seen on Arctiria, but it was torn open in places, revealing more battered circuitry beneath. Its red hair hung from its scalp in clumps. He ran, heart pounding in his throat.

A figure appeared in front of him, blocking the door to the brig. A familiar figure.

Max skidded to a halt.

"Hello, nephew," said the Professor. "I had

a feeling I'd find you sniffing around down here."

In his hand he held a blaster pistol. He levelled it at Max.

With nowhere to go, Max took a deep breath. "Tell me where my real mum is!" he said. "You've got her somewhere, haven't you? Otherwise you couldn't have made the clone."

The Professor smiled, his eyes twinkling. "You're hardly in a position to make demands," he said. "I'm afraid my little invention will have to make do for now. She was quite badly damaged from that fall, but it gave me the opportunity to make some… adjustments. Why not take a look?"

Max turned back to the clone. It raised its arms, and with a whirring sound both hands folded into its wrists. In their place emerged a gleaming hyperblade and an ice pick.

It came towards him with slow, steady steps, swishing its weapons from side to side.

"I don't think I can watch," said the Professor. "Too much blood makes me feel queasy!"

Max raised his hands to fight, but he knew it was a useless gesture. He didn't have a chance.

A cavity opened in the clone's chest and – *SNAP!* – a metal cord shot out and wrapped around Max's middle, pinning his arms to his side. Gears whirred and the cord began to pull him closer to the clone. Max struggled, but it only bound him more tightly.

It can't end like this, he thought suddenly. *I've looked for her for so long and now her clone is going to kill me!*

"Goodbye, Max," said the Professor.

The clone bared its jaws in something like a grin, raised the hyperblade, and…

WHACK!

A metal bar connected with the side of its head, splitting open its neck in a tangle of wires. The clone slumped to the ground. Behind it stood another figure.

"Leave my boy alone."

Max's saviour pushed her long hair back, revealing a face streaked with dirt and grime.

In that moment, Max knew for sure. The clone had looked just like he'd imagined his mother would – a snapshot of a young woman. This woman was older, harder, stronger. Her face was lined. But none of that mattered, because it was her.

"Mum," he whispered.

Her eyes suddenly widened. "Duck!" she shouted.

Max crouched and she threw the metal bar, spinning through the air. Max heard a thump and a cry of pain and turned to see the Professor sinking to the ground, bleeding from a cut on his head. His blaster hung limply in his hand.

His mum stepped over the fallen clone, and opened her arms.

"Now, how about that hug?" she said.

CHAPTER FOUR

HOSTAGE SITUATION

Max threw himself into his mum's arms. "I thought I'd never see you again," she said, her voice choked with emotion. She held him so tightly he could hardly breathe.

"I never gave up hope," said Max. "Everyone said you had to be dead, but I knew you were out here somewhere."

He pulled himself away so he could look into her face. Though there were lines there now, her eyes were the same blue he

had imagined – kind and gentle. But then something else caught his attention. The gill-slits on her neck. *She's got the Merryn Touch, just like me.*

He lifted his chin to show her, and she gasped. "How…? Who? I don't understand."

"It's a long story, Mum," Max said.

"And Callum?" she asked, her lip trembling.

Max smiled. "He's here on a ship, fighting Cora. We have to stop her before she destroys the defence shield and finds the last key for the Kraken's Eye!"

"Don't worry, I know Cora's plan," said his mother, rolling her eyes. "My brother has delighted in explaining every detail to me."

The clone twitched on the floor, then lay still.

"How did you get out?" asked Max. He could hardly believe it was her. Real. In the flesh. Around her neck he saw a blue crystal pendant that triggered distant memories. He recalled her wearing it when he was little, remembered reaching for it with his hands…

His mother shrugged. "I was in a special cell, protected by an electronic force-field. For some reason it just switched off."

Max smiled to himself. "Our friend Roger killed the power."

"Not Roger the pirate?" said his mother, looking alarmed. "Long grey hair, wears an eye patch? What's that scoundrel doing here?"

"It's a long story," said Max. "But he's on our side, I promise."

His mother pressed her lips together, looking unconvinced. "If you say so." She nodded at her brother, who was still lying unconscious on the ground. "Let's get him out of the way." Together, they dragged his body into the cell where the clone had been. His mother took the Professor's blaster and tucked it in her belt, while Max retrieved his hyperblade. Next, they pushed the clone in with him. Sparks fizzed across its skin, making Max shudder.

As they locked the door, the Professor stirred on the floor with a groan. He shook his head in confusion, then his eyes widened as he saw the clone, which was beginning to judder wildly. "What are you doing?" he wailed. "You can't leave me in here with that…thing."

The clone suddenly sat up, and swiped the ice pick in a wide arc. The Professor dodged back against the wall.

"Do you think he'll be OK?" Max asked, as they walked away. His mother didn't even

look at her brother.

"I expect so. The clone's not fully functional."

The Professor's shouts faded as they rounded the corner.

"My brother and I never really got on," said Max's mum quietly. "He was always so ambitious and determined. But I couldn't have known how evil he would become."

The ship's intercom crackled and hissed from a speaker on the ceiling. "Listen up, crew," said Cora's voice. "I want that Merryn girl brought to me alive. Anyone who takes matters into their own hands will feel the sting of the cat, understand?"

"There are Merryn on board?" asked Max's mother. "How is that possible?"

"My friend Lia," said Max. "She wears an Amphibio mask." He pointed to his gills. "Lia saved my life when I was drowning."

The speakers crackled again. "We've got the little bilge-rat!" said a voice. "Bringing her to the bridge now."

Max's heart leaped into his throat. "No!" he said. "We have to rescue her!"

"Follow me!" said his mother. They hurried down several corridors until they reached a lift shaft, where she pressed a button.

As the lift rumbled upwards, Max's mother looked down at him. "I can't believe it's you," she said. "You were only two years old when I left – just toddling around."

Max felt himself blushing.

According to the lift display, they were nearly at the bridge. Max's mother pulled out the blaster pistol and checked the charge. Max brandished his hyperblade. *We're ready for you, Cora...*

As the doors swished open they stepped out onto a balcony, overlooking the *Pride of Blackheart*'s control deck. A wide viewing screen looked out over the battle, and monitors flashed with alerts and diagnostic reports. The whole room quaked each time the ship's massive guns fired. In the centre of the bridge sat Lia, hands bound behind her back and ankles tied together. Max was glad to see she still had her Amphibio mask on.

Cora stood in front of her, flanked by four pirates and armed with her electric cat-o'-nine-tails.

"I'll ask you one more time," she said to Lia. "Tell me where the keys are, or I'll flay the skin from your back."

Lia glared at Cora, but she didn't speak.

"Very well," said Cora. "Let's see how stubborn you can really be..." She raised the whip, and blue sparks crackled from it.

"Stop!" shouted Max. Raising his hyperblade, he placed one hand on the balcony railing and vaulted over the top. He landed heavily in front of Cora.

The pirate smiled. "You heroes are so predictable," she said. "You've walked right into my trap!"

Each of the four pirates drew electric blades and fanned out around him.

I've made a terrible mistake, thought Max.

CHAPTER FIVE

ROGER'S BLACKMAIL

"Stretch and Stinky…kill him!" snapped Cora.

Two pirates closed in. Max didn't need to ask which was which. Stretch towered over everyone in the room, but his limbs were skinny, like dangling wires. Max could smell Stinky from ten paces – the eggy stench of seaweed left in the sun too long.

He took a step back and raised his hyperblade. As Stinky swung her sword, Max blocked and tripped him with a swipe of his leg. Then he turned to Stretch. Too late. A blow sent his hyperblade spinning out of his hand. Stretch leaned closer. "I'll just give him a little scratch," he said, jabbing his glowing sword-tip towards Max's face.

Max flinched, but just before the point scarred his cheek Stretch doubled over as Max's mother kicked him in the stomach. The other two pirates leaped onto her at once and pinned her arms behind her back.

"What a pleasant surprise," said Cora. "The boy *and* his adoring mother! I told my engineer – that's your dear brother, by the way – we should have killed you long ago."

Stretch climbed to his feet, while Stinky reclaimed her blade. Both looked sheepish as they pointed their weapons at Max, forcing him back against a console. *Nowhere to run.*

Max's mother glared at Cora. "You'll find

your 'engineer' in the brig, by the way. Where you *both* belong."

Cora tipped back her head and laughed. She strode towards Max's mother, and for a moment Max thought she would strike her. Instead, she reached to her neck and ripped

the blue pendant off by its chain. "Pretty!" she said. "I'm sure your boy was smart enough not to bring the keys here for me... So I'll have this as a consolation prize!"

"Give that back!" said Max's mum.

Cora ignored her, turning on her robotic peg leg to face the large screen on one side of the bridge.

Max hated to see his mother lose her pendant. *Still, it's lucky I sent the keys away with Rivet...* He cast a glance around. Where was Roger? They needed his help!

Leaning over a control panel, Cora pressed a few buttons and the screen zoomed in on the battle-scarred city, showing the devastation in close-up. Smoke trailed from the sides of the skyscrapers and debris filled the shoreline. An Aquoran cruiser was nose-down in the water, sinking. Several Gustadian vessels were damaged too. Thankfully, the defence shield seemed to have held. Troops lined the top, firing at the *Blackheart*'s subs in the water below.

"You'll never get into Aquora," said Max's mum. "My husband will defend our city to the last man."

"Brave words," said Cora, "but we haven't even unleashed our secret weapon yet. Look!"

As they stared at the screen, the water stirred near the shoreline and Chakrol's hammerhead breached the surface. It swam straight towards an Aquoran sailor flailing in the shallows and snatched him up in its mouth. Max couldn't watch, but he heard the sailor's screams quickly rise and fade.

"You're a monster," said Lia.

"Oh, that was just an appetiser," said Cora. "Let's see how your pathetic shield stands up to Chakrol!"

She pressed another button, and Chakrol's

rocket launchers loaded and swivelled to face the defensive wall. Two missiles fizzed through the air and collided with the titanium shield with a sound like thunder. A huge wave swelled up and the *Pride of Blackheart* shook with the power of the explosion.

When the smoke cleared, Max gasped in horror. The missiles had blown a small hole in the shield and heavily dented the area around it. Bodies floated in the water below.

The screen suddenly cut out in static.

"What's going on?" said Cora.

A picture flickered into view. A face. One eye, and the other covered in a patch...

"Roger!" exclaimed Max, his mother and Cora in unison.

Roger grinned into the camera. "Right, is this working? Have I got your attention?"

Cora pressed a communicator switch on her tunic. "Where are you, traitor? I'll have you keel-hauled, you slippery eel!"

"Steady on, old girl," said Roger. "That's no way to greet your old crewmate, is it?"

So he wasn't lying, Max thought. *Roger really used to sail with Cora Blackheart.*

Cora pointed to Stinky and Stretch. "Find him! Bring him to me!"

Roger grinned. "Calm down," he said. "I'll show you where I am."

The camera angle changed and Max

realised that Roger must be holding the recording device in his hand. Max saw a beautiful statue of Thallos, the sea creature god of the Merryn people, carved from coral. Then a chest, with gold coins piled higher than the rim. Then a tall vase, just like one Max had seen in Arctiria.

"He's in the treasure hold!" gasped Stretch.

Cora's skin went deathly pale, and her cheeks twitched with fury.

The screen showed more precious treasures from the seas of Nemos. A diamond the size of a fist glinted so brightly it hurt Max's eyes.

"Is that the Scurvy Diamond of Hulvado?" said his mum. "I thought it was just a legend."

"How did that filthy cur get in there?" Cora muttered.

"Once a pirate, always a pirate," said Roger, turning the camera back to his face. "Looks like I've outsmarted you this time, eh, Cora?"

But Max noticed the flicker of a smile on the pirate captain's lips.

"Well, Roger, you're in a room with only one exit and my men are on their way," said Cora. "So enjoy your booty until they arrive. After that, I'm afraid you're shark food."

Roger didn't look scared. "You see, I thought you might say that, which is why I brought my back-up plan along."

The camera turned again to Roger's free hand. He was holding a marine grenade.

"This little beauty should be enough to blow all your treasure to smithereens, and leave a nice big hole in the side of your ship at the same time."

Cora sucked in a breath and steadied herself against the control console. "You wouldn't!"

Roger's face filled the screen, deadly serious. "Oh, I would," he said. "So listen up, Cora. Release my friends, or this lot goes to the bottom of the ocean. All your loot, collected over the years, up in smoke. Got it?"

Max shared a glance with Lia. Cora was distracted. And that meant for the time being they had an advantage… Max looked around for a weapon, but his hyperblade was out of reach. There was nothing else. Perhaps he could scramble some wiring to cause a distraction? He checked. No, all the control panels were screwed shut.

"Please! No!" wailed Cora. "How can you call yourself a pirate?"

Max's eyes landed on Cora's robotic leg, just out of arm's reach.

The circuitry looked simple enough. *If I can get close enough…*

Cora was busy watching the screen.

Max seized the moment and leaped at her, knocking her to the ground. "Argh! What are you doing, you bilge rat?" yelled Cora. Max grabbed her peg leg, fingers rooting into the circuitry. He sensed Stretch and Stinky closing in. *No more than a few seconds…* He found the right switch, and deactivated it.

"Get him off me!" shouted Cora. A hand grabbed Max's leg and another closed around the back of his neck. He focused all his attention on tweaking the wiring. Just before the pirates pulled him away, he leaned forward and whispered a single word into the leg's voice activators: "Dance."

Cora scrambled up and glared at Max. "Getting rather desperate, aren't you?"

Max said nothing. He just hoped his reprogramming had worked. And that he had a chance to test it out…

"Bring them to me," Roger was saying. "If you're not here in five minutes, it's goodbye treasure."

At his words, the screen filled with static.

CHAPTER SIX

CHALLENGING CHAKROL

Cora's pirates looked at their captain, waiting for instructions.

She growled, deep in her throat. "We have to do as he says! Stretch, stay here and take charge of the attack on Aquora. I'll deal with Roger." She turned to Max. "And don't you worry, he won't be called *Jolly* Roger when I'm finished with him!"

Cora led Lia, Max and his mother into a lift, escorted by the three other pirates. Max watched the floors tick by:

Deck Level, -1, -2, Water Level, -3, -4…

He wondered if his leg reprogramming had even worked. But he couldn't risk finding out yet. If he used it at the wrong time, it would be wasted. *I need to pick the perfect moment…*

At the fifth level below deck, Cora pressed the red STOP button and the lift juddered to a halt. The door opened onto a narrow, low-ceilinged corridor.

"Move it, you lot," Cora snapped.

Max stepped out first, followed by Lia and his mother. The pirates came next, and Cora brought up the rear.

At the end of the passage was a round steel door, wide open. Roger leaned against the doorway, grenade in his one good hand and his hook through the pin. Behind him, Max could see the treasure hold.

"Better not come any closer, Cora," Roger

said, grinning. "You wouldn't want me to panic and pull this out!"

"You always were a sneaky snake," snarled Cora.

"You were the one who mutinied and left me stuck on a desert island," Roger replied.

Max looked back and forth between them in amazement. *So that's how they parted ways!*

"You deserved it, *Captain*!" Cora shot back.

"Your crew thought you were a fool!"

"I've still got permanent tan-lines from the sunburn!" Roger said, looking hurt.

"My heart bleeds," said Cora. "If I had my way, the crabs would have—"

"Ahem," Max interrupted. "Maybe we should be leaving. Wasn't that the plan?"

Roger grinned. "Right you are, m'lad. Off you go. Cora and I have a lot to discuss."

Cora smiled too, but her eyes sparkled with hatred. "Yes, run along. But you'd better run quickly. As soon as I've dealt with this traitor I'll be coming after you."

Max nodded and called out to Roger. "You're the bravest pirate I've ever met."

Roger nodded. "And the most handsome too. Good luck, Max."

Leaving the pirates in their stand-off, Max, Lia and his mother ran back to the lift.

"We have to get off the ship," said Max.

"And I know just the way." He pressed the button which said *Level -6: Docking Bay*.

When the doors opened again, they came out into a room with a steel mesh floor and submarine pods lined up on one side. Most were empty, no doubt taken by pirates for the assault on Aquora. But the last few weren't. They passed Cora's personal sub, with a black heart on the side. It was a refitted Quadrant vessel, an Intercept-Destroy model, or QID for short. Max was sorely tempted to steal it, but they'd need something bigger for the three of them.

A few pods along they came to a Quadrant Exploration and Reconnaissance Vessel, or QERV. It wouldn't be as quick, but Max saw that the pirates had fitted it with weaponry and there was plenty of room inside. And it was daubed with a skull and crossbones, just like all the others.

"The pirates certainly made themselves at home, didn't they?" said Max's mum.

"We can sneak up on them," said Lia. "They'll think we're pirates too."

Max pressed a few buttons and the sub's hatch slid open.

"Let's go," he said.

They clambered in, Max sliding into the pilot's position and engaging the engines.

The QERV's launch threw them back in their seats as they blasted out into the open sea. Straightaway Max found himself in the middle of a battle. Pirate QIDs and Aquoran Defence subs zipped through the water, exchanging fire. Max saw a Sea Lion ZX200, just like the one he'd taken to go after his father when he was first kidnapped by the Professor. This one trailed smoke as it crashed towards the seabed. Above, the dark shapes of battleships and frigates moved across the surface. The boom of their guns shook the sea like underwater thunder.

Max pressed his communicator. "Dad, can you hear me?"

After a crackle, the channel became clear. "Max! Thank goodness you're still alive. Where are you, son?"

"We've stolen one of Cora's QERVs," Max replied. "Tell your people not to fire at us.

We're going to sneak up on the pirates."

"Will do, Max. But hurry. The defence shield is almost down. We haven't got long."

Max paused for a moment, then looked at his mother. Her eyes were misty. *Should I tell him who I've found?*

"Dad," he said. "You'll never guess who…" The line went dead. "Dad?"

Nothing.

Lia pointed at the screen, off to the left, where four QIDs were surrounding an Aquoran defence sub. "Let's go and help!"

Max steered the QERV over, but he couldn't see how to control the weapons. His mum peered over his shoulder. "Use the flares," she said. "The pirates have adapted them into heat-seeking rockets." Max slammed the red flare button and the rockets armed.

The Aquoran sub was under heavy attack, taking blasts from both sides. Max sent two

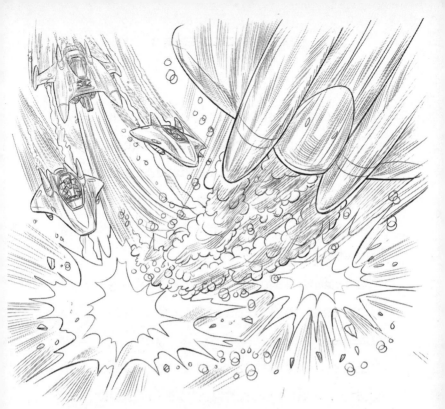

rockets scorching through the water. The two nearest QIDs exploded in flashes of light. The remaining pirate sub turned and opened fire. Max rolled the QERV and the blasters passed by harmlessly. It gave the Aquoran sub time to right itself. With a couple of well-aimed torpedoes, another QID went spinning into the depths. The remaining pirate, outnumbered and outgunned, gave up and sped away.

The Aquoran sub skimmed through the water alongside them. Its hull was scarred and dented, but not broken. Through the viewing screen Max saw his father at the controls, grinning.

"Nice shooting, Dad!" said Max.

"You too, son!" replied Callum. "Now what were you trying to tell me before?"

As he spoke, Max's mother leaned right up to the viewing screen and looked out. Max saw his dad's face grow pale.

"Niobe…" he said in a whisper.

His mother swallowed. "It's me, Callum. I've…missed you."

BOOM!

The water around them shook.

"What was that?" asked Lia.

"The defence wall has just gone down," said Callum. His eyes bored into Max's. "Son, we need to stop the Robobeast. The future of Aquora hangs in the balance."

"Not just Aquora," said Max. "The future of all Nemos." Lia squeezed his arm. He smiled at her, trying to look confident. "We have to go after Chakrol. See you when all this is over, Dad."

At least, I hope so…

CHAPTER SEVEN

AT THE ROBOBEAST'S MERCY

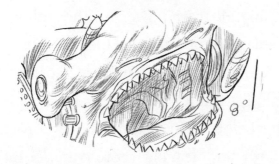

"We can't let Chakrol destroy the shield," Max said, steering the QERV towards the shoreline. Huge sections of the titanium wall had toppled into the water among the other debris. There were fragments of ships, and injured Aquorans swimming for safety.

Max's grip tightened on the controls. *So many innocent lives lost already…*

As Max brought the QERV to the surface he saw Chakrol. The top half of the hammerhead shark reared out of the water, lurching onto land. *What's it doing? It'll beach itself!* The Aquoran defenders were focusing all their power on the Robobeast. Two blaster cannons were blazing away from the remains of the titanium defence shield, and brave soldiers were firing blaster pistols from below. The cannons were rocking Chakrol and leaving scorch marks on its side, but the soldiers might as well have been shooting peas from a blowpipe.

"It's stuck," said Lia. "It can't get back in the water."

"I don't think it wants to," said Max's mum.

Almost as soon as she had spoken, panels opened on the Robobeast's underbelly, and several pairs of mechanical legs sprouted out. With a grinding sound, the monster began to heave itself onto land.

My uncle's thought of everything, thought Max grimly.

Max scanned the QERV's controls, and found what he was looking for – a grappling hook. He took aim at Chakrol's back leg and fired. The sub jolted as a large hook on a steel cord shot from its bow. The cord wrapped itself around the Robobeast's leg and locked firm. Max switched the thrusters to reverse, maximum power. The engines screamed and frothed up the water, and Chakrol's leg slipped from underneath him. The Robobeast flopped into the water, throwing up spray. But almost straight away it lifted its leg again, yanking the QERV through the water and snapping the grappling cable like cotton thread.

Heart racing, Max scanned the baffling array of controls. *What is there that can possibly stop a Robobeast that size?*

His mum slid into the seat beside him. "Give me some room. I know these QERVs better than you."

"It had just better have a very big gun somewhere," muttered Max.

His mother shook her head. "It's got something much more useful."

She flicked a switch that read *IDD* and a cross hair appeared in the screen.

"What's IDD?" asked Max.

"Internal Diagnostic Dart," replied his mum. She aimed the cross hair over the Robobeast's flank and fired.

Something shot from the QERV. It looked like a sleek torpedo, no longer than Max's forearm. With a soft thunk, it buried itself in Chakrol's side, and at once, the corner of the screen began to show an image of circuitry and flashing robotics in the shape of a hammerhead shark.

"The IDD scans tech systems," said Max's mum. "And if we know *how* it works…"

"…maybe we can stop it," Max finished. "Mum, you're a genius!"

As they watched, Chakrol dragged itself further out of the water. Water poured off its flanks, charred from the defenders' bombardment. Max saw that metal plates had extended over its gills as well – no doubt allowing it to breathe out of water. With a shake of its head, it battered down another section of the shield. Soldiers leaped into the water, screaming.

"Concentrate fire on the other back leg!" said Max to his dad through his communicator. "We need to slow it down."

"Got you," said Callum. He gunned his sub closer and opened fire on the leg. Smoke and flashes filled the water. Max drummed his fingers impatiently on the control panel as he watched the scan develop. The circuits were incredible because of their size, but

the tech wasn't complicated. And it looked like the control hub, the robotic brain, was in the back of Chakrol's throat. *That's just like the Professor…* If Max could reach it and disengage the main power cable, Chakrol would be free from his uncle's control.

But if it sees me coming, I'm lunch!

Max set the QERV's guns to lock on the leg and maintain fire. He turned and saw Lia sitting at the back of the vessel, arms wrapped round her legs, mumbling to herself.

"What are you doing?" he asked. "We need all hands on deck here!"

She seemed not to hear him.

"Lia!" he shouted.

This time her eyes rose to meet his, but they were unfocused, as though she was looking right through him.

Great! Now she loses her nerve! But there was nothing he could do about it.

Max returned his attention to the screen. Callum was edging closer, firing every few seconds at the Robobeast's leg. Parts of the metal were beginning to buckle and melt.

It's working. If we can just keep this up…

WHAM! With a sudden twitch, Chakrol's reinforced tail slammed into his dad's sub. The power was incredible, and Max saw the craft split into pieces. His dad spun free in the water, still attached to his seat.

"Callum!" gasped Max's mum.

"Dad!" Max yelled.

For a moment, Max feared the worst, but then he saw his dad shaking his head, as if to clear his senses, and quickly strapping on an Amphibio mask.

Chakrol seemed to have forgotten his mission to get on shore. He turned and pushed through the water, snapping up the remains of Callum's vessel, then gliding towards Max's dad himself...

Max's skin crawled as he watched his father struggling to unfasten his safety harness. Chakrol stalked closer with menacing slowness.

His dad was a sitting duck. And there was nothing anyone could do to save him.

CHAPTER EIGHT

INTO THE MAW

Max steered the QERV up towards the surface, then rushed to the airlock.

"Max, wait!" said Lia, suddenly coming to life again and gripping his arm.

He shook her off. "There's no time. Dad's going to be shark food unless I get out there."

"No, he won't," said Lia. "Look!"

She was pointing at the screen showing the QERV's rear view, out to sea. As Max flashed a glance in that direction, he couldn't believe what he was seeing.

It can't be…

A long reptilian snout slid into view from the black depths, lined with sharp teeth.

"Tetrax!" said Max, recognising the crocodile they'd freed from the Professor's robotics. A tingle of fear went up his spine. "What's he doing here?"

"Keep looking," said Lia.

Another huge shadow approached, this time from the left – a thick coil of scaly flesh uncurling from the deep. A giant sea serpent.

"Is that Finaria?" said Max. *Two more Robobeasts to face – this can't be happening!*

Last of all came Nephro, its massive lobster claws snatching at the water as its armoured shell rose towards Chakrol from the right side. To Max's relief, none of the creatures had any sign of their old robotic enhancements.

"I don't understand," said Max.

"That's because you've been so busy with

your *tech*," said Lia. She folded her arms proudly. "I called to them with my Aqua Powers. They're angry with the Professor. They're on *our* side!"

So that was what all the rumbling was about!

With three huge sea creatures bearing down on it, Chakrol left Max's dad floating there and turned to face the new threats. Callum had just managed to escape from his seat.

"Dad!" Max said into his communicator. "Get over to our sub! Quickly!"

His father began to swim towards them, just as Finaria's head slipped beneath Chakrol's belly. The serpent's muscular body wrapped silently around the shark Robobeast, then began to tighten. Chakrol's hammerhead thrashed, but he couldn't throw the serpent off. Next Tetrax's jaws closed around the robotics on the Robobeast's tail. Max felt like a sardine watching sharks do battle.

"You did it!" he said. "You saved my dad!"

Callum made it to the airlock and clambered into their vessel, dripping wet. "I owe you both a big thank you!" he said. "I thought that was it for…" His words dried up as he stood gazing at Max's mother. She was still hanging back, as if unsure what to do. Callum's mouth opened and closed silently. Then he managed

to speak. "Niobe," he said simply.

Without a word, she ran into his arms.

The sound of tearing metal drew Max's eyes back to the screen. Outside, Chakrol was squirming in the water, trying to avoid Nephro's bone-crushing claws. At least one of its metal gill-plates had been ripped off already. Max saw deep cuts in the lobster's side where the Robobeast must have got its teeth in. Thrashing his head, Chakrol slammed Tetrax in the jaw. The huge crocodile rolled over in the water, dazed. Finaria reared back, ready to strike, but Chakrol whipped around its tail and clubbed the serpent brutally.

"They won't be able to hold Chakrol off forever," murmured Max. "It's too powerful with all of the Professor's additions." He climbed the ladder to the hatch himself.

"No!" said his mum and dad together.

Max pointed to his gills. "It has to be me. I know the robotics, and I can swim without being detected." He tried a smile to hide his fear. "Trust me. I've done this before."

Before they could stop him, he broke open the hatch and climbed on top of the floating sub. Clouds of smoke and the smell of burning hung over Aquora's coast, and the remains of several ships floated on the oil-slicked surface.

Just ahead, he saw Chakrol's top half burst from the waves. He had Nephro in his jaws, and the giant lobster's claws waved around helplessly. Tetrax was clinging to one side of Chakrol's hammerhead, his body dangling below.

They're fighting bravely, but it's not enough, thought Max. *No time to waste.*

He plunged off the sub in a steep dive and the water closed over him with a splash.

It was hard to make out what was happening as the four Beasts battled. Max swam quickly into the heart of the fight, trying not to worry about getting eaten or torn apart. There were trails of blood from the good Beasts, which bellowed and roared in pain and anger. Max ducked beneath one of Nephro's antennae, then almost got swatted by Tetrax's tail. In a clearer patch of water, he saw Chakrol's yawning mouth and kicked towards it.

The safest place right now is inside that

Robobeast's jaws!

Chakrol spotted him. Max froze as the Beast lurched towards him, teeth bared.

A split second before certain death, Finaria's head slammed into the shark's, butting it aside and leaving it dazed. Max saw his chance and swam into the Robobeast's mouth. He kicked as hard as he could past the looming rows of jagged teeth emerging from pink gums.

Suddenly Chakrol's head shook wildly, throwing Max from side to side.

He must know I'm in here!

Max winced as he smashed into the nearest tooth and it cut his side. Now his blood mixed with the blood of the Beasts in the water.

He ignored the pain and pushed off the tooth, further into the Robobeast's gloomy throat. He saw the glow of circuitry ahead, huge cables and sensors embedded in Chakrol's flesh, tapping into the creature's nervous system. There was a box in the centre that sprouted dozens of wires.

The control hub.

Suddenly everything went dark as Chakrol closed its mouth.

"Your last line of defence," Max muttered. "But you won't beat me!"

He reached out and swam towards the control box until his fingers found the edge. Now, which wire was it? Max closed his eyes, trying to remember the map he'd seen in the QERV. *If I pull the wrong wire, the whole Robobeast might self-destruct with me inside it!*

He felt the wires leading into the hub.

Not that one…

Or that one…

Thoughts of his mother and father and Lia filled his head. And the people of Aquora, his home. *I can't let them all down…*

Max fought to clear his mind as his fingers found the cable he was looking for. *Here goes...*

Bracing himself, he yanked with all his might, and the cable tore free in a flash of blue sparks.

FFFFRRRRMmmmm.

For an instant, light filled the cavernous throat, and the tech made a whirring sound as it powered down. Then other pieces of circuitry began to fall away from the beast's flesh.

Had it really worked?

With a tremendous sucking sensation, Max felt himself being hurled out into open sea, together with all the robotic debris. His ankle got caught and he went spinning upside down. When he finally managed to look up, he found that he was dangling from Nephro's claw.

"Good catch!" said Max as the lobster gently released him.

Looking back, he saw that Chakrol's coughing had dislodged all the Professor's tech. Its robotic legs and armour plating began to fall away too, in streaming clouds of bubbles.

The vast hammerhead shark looked almost as if it was smiling.

Chakrol is free!

As Max marvelled at the sight, the QERV pulled up alongside him.

"Great work, son!" said his dad through the communicator. "But we're not finished yet. There's one more job to do…"

A STING IN THE TAIL

They were crowded into a lift, shooting high up a skyscraper on Aquora – Lia, Max and his mum and dad.

"I hope Roger's all right," said Max. "Without him we'd all be dead."

"There'll be time to rescue Roger later," said Niobe. "Right now, Cora has a lot more to worry about than one pesky pirate."

The floors slipped past too quickly to count. Max noticed that his mum and dad were holding hands tightly, their knuckles white, as if afraid to let go of each other again. Lia looked a little green under her Amphibio mask.

"I don't like heights," she muttered. "Depths are OK, but heights..."

Max's dad was speaking fast into his communicator, giving orders. "Send a boarding party onto the *Blackheart*! Take all the pirates prisoner. But be careful – Cora Blackheart won't come easily."

At Level 200 the lift lurched to a halt, making Max's stomach yo-yo to his throat and back.

They stepped out into the most incredible lab Max had ever seen. It covered the entire floor of the skyscraper, and every surface was of gleaming steel. Banks of monitors showed charts and read-outs, while others displayed views of the city from different security cameras. Huge machines flashed symbols he didn't understand. Men and women in white coats moved silently through the space. They seemed so calm considering the carnage below.

"Welcome to the Innovation Department," said Callum. "This place is top secret, but I think you've earned the right to see it."

"Pretty cool, huh?" Max said to Lia.

She was staring, goggle-eyed, at some sort of liquid metal in a vertical tube. Next to it, a scientist wearing goggles was tapping at a computer screen. Each time he did, the metal moved like treacle, catching the light and re-forming into different shapes. "Not bad," Lia admitted. "For technology, anyway."

Max grinned. He could tell from her wide eyes that even she was impressed.

A metallic bark made Max spin round, and he saw Rivet bound over and raise himself up on his hind paws. "Max safe! Rivet hero!"

"Yes, you are!" said Max, patting Rivet's head. "It's good to see you again, Riv."

Callum led them towards a glass tank, empty except for a raised platform inside it. He slid open the side of the tank.

"The Kraken's Eye was created for good," he said, "but we should have known the temptation to use it would have been too great for some. Do you have the keys?"

Max reached down and opened Rivet's back compartment. There they were, safe and sound – the keys of Gustados, Arctiria and Verdula.

"Where's the Aquoran one?" Max asked.

His dad gave a mischievous smile and reached under his uniform, pulling out a metal chain from around his neck. The key was dangling on the end.

"You had it all along!" said Max.

"I needed to know exactly where it was," said his dad. "If Aquora had fallen, I would have taken it to the deepest part of the ocean and thrown it away." He placed the four keys inside the tank, on top of the platform, then closed the side panel. "This vaporiser breaks matter down at atomic level. Hit that red button on the control panel, would you, Niobe?" he said.

"Not so fast," came a voice across the room.

Everyone turned as Cora Blackheart and Max's uncle stepped from the lift. Both were holding blasters. Max's heart jolted, then sank. If there were two faces he'd hoped never to see again, it was these two. Somehow, they must have slipped through the Aquoran defences. *We've come all this way. It can't end like this…*

"Sorry to interrupt the family reunion," said his uncle, "but someone forgot to invite me."

Max saw the Professor had a huge lump on his head and was covered in scratches, no doubt from his battle with the clone.

"But…how did you get out?" asked Lia.

The Professor's lip curled into a snarl.

"I let him out, you idiot," said Cora.

"But what about Roger's bomb?" said Max.

"I called his bluff," said Cora. "You didn't really think Roger...a pirate...could bring himself to destroy all that treasure, did you? He's back in the brig, where he belongs. But I'm feeling merciful. After I've got the keys, I'll let him go. He can stay here and enjoy life. Well, for a few minutes...until I wipe Aquora off the charts with the Kraken's Eye!" The expression on her face told Max she was deadly serious.

"Now," said his uncle. "Give me those keys."

Max saw the look of panic in his parents' eyes. None of them were armed, and the scientists didn't have any weapons either. *We can't let them have the keys now.*

Max's eyes went to the red button that would destroy the keys. It was a few paces away. He edged closer, but the Professor's gun followed him. "Freeze, nephew," he said.

Cora stepped closer and pointed her blaster at Callum. "Give. Me. The. Keys."

Then Max remembered. *The peg leg!*

"Dance!" he yelled. He just hoped his

reprogramming had worked…

For a moment, nothing happened. Then a look of shock crossed Cora's face as her leg suddenly shot sideways from under her and started to dance a jig of its own accord. *Tap-tap-tappety-tap.*

"What's going on?" she yelled. She dropped her gun and tried to grab at her leg, but it jerked away wildly.

The Professor was gaping at Cora. This was it. *Now or never.* Max leaped and slammed his palm down on the red button.

Everything seemed to happen at once. The machine began to hum as a white laser beam fired onto the keys. Rivet launched himself across the lab and clamped his teeth over the Professor's wrist. His uncle's blaster went off target and a huge section of the window cracked and exploded outwards. A sudden gust of wind whipped through the lab, scattering papers and knocking over equipment.

The vaporiser's hum rose in pitch to a whine, and the light inside suddenly flashed and died.

Max peered closer, his heart thumping. The keys were gone, and a small cloud of smoke hung in the air of the tank.

"Make it stop!" cried Cora. She was thrashing on the floor now.

"I don't know how," said Max. He couldn't

help laughing with relief. "I didn't have time to programme that."

"The Kraken's Eye is no use to anyone now," said Callum, putting an arm around Max's mum. The Professor was standing against a wall, guarded by a snarling Rivet. He was scowling, and clutching his wrist where Rivet had bitten him.

Max grinned at Lia. "We did it!" he said. She raised a webbed hand and they high-fived.

At last Cora managed to detach her leg and scramble up onto her one good foot.

"It's over, Cora," said Max. "There's nowhere to run."

The pirate's eyes flashed around the room in anger. "That's what you think," she said. She began to hop towards the open window.

"Wait! No!" said Callum. "It's two hundred storeys—"

Cora flung herself from the window.

Max's heart raced as he and Lia ran to the opening. He saw Cora's body angled into a straight dive. It became a dot as she plummeted far below towards the sea. Then she entered the water with barely a splash.

"She must be dead, surely," said Niobe. "No one could survive a dive from this height!"

Max looked at his dad's pale face. "No one," he said, a hint of uncertainty in his voice.

Guards arrived in the lift and surrounded Max's uncle. "I can't believe she abandoned me," said the Professor glumly.

"Take him to a holding cell," said Callum. "He'll be charged with high treason against the city of Aquora, and crimes against Nemos."

The Professor fought as the guards seized him and bundled him into the lift. "You haven't heard the last of me!" he yelled. "I'll be back, I promise you!"

The lift doors closed, swallowing his cries.

CHAPTER TEN

NEW PERILS

As the afternoon sun sank towards the horizon, Max stood at the window of his old apartment on Level 523. Below, the repair work was already in progress. Huge cranes hoisted bits of damaged buildings out of the roads. Teams of workmen cleared debris and laid new cables. Elsewhere, a group with soldering irons were reinforcing the defence wall. Cora and Chakrol's bombardment had caused huge damage, but Max knew the city would survive if everyone pulled together.

Further out of the harbour, salvage vessels were towing damaged ships back towards the jetties. The pirates on board the *Pride of Blackheart* had surrendered soon after the Beasts – Tetrax, Nephro, Finaria and Chakrol – had disappeared into the depths. Now the vessel was at anchor while Aquoran defence officers led captured pirates off to prison.

Soldiers had hunted high and low for Cora's body, but nothing had been found. There were reports of a break-in on the lower decks of the *Blackheart*, and even an explosion, but no one was sure if anything had gone missing. Max had a bad feeling about it, but there was no point worrying about the future. If Cora returned, he would be ready for her.

Lia arrived at Max's side, still breathing through her Amphibio mask.

"Any word on Roger?" Max asked.

She shook her head. "Nothing, but I found this in the brig." She held up a small waterproof sack, with 'For Niobe' stitched on the outside. Frowning, Max tipped the contents out into his hand. It contained a brooch, silver by the look of it, with a sparkling green gem in the centre.

"It must be from the treasure chamber," said Max. *But why would Roger want to give this to my mum?* Maybe the old pirate had a soft spot for her.

"If I know Roger," said Lia, "he's up to mischief somewhere."

Rivet barked from beside Max's leg.

"Hungry, Max! Rivet eat!"

Max touched a few buttons on the control panel by the window, and a dog bowl with Rivet's name slid out of the wall on wheels and scooted towards them.

"Yum! Yum!" said Rivet.

Max grinned and whispered to Lia. "It's a mixture of oil and grease, plus a couple of real dog biscuits. I think it makes him feel at home."

As Rivet nosed around in the bowl, Max felt Lia looking at him intently.

"And what about you?" she asked. "Now the Quest is over, do you feel at home?"

Max turned to look around his father's sleek apartment. Touchscreens and state-of-the-art tech had been concealed in just about every piece of furniture, from the seats that could massage and read books to you, to the windows that could scroll the news headlines. The nutrition console could create any dish known to man. He'd grown up here, a sheltered life high in the clouds, where nothing could touch him. But...

He looked at Lia. This place was about as different from her home city of Sumara as was possible. The Merryn people lived at one with nature, sculpting plants and coral to form their houses and streets, using their Aqua Powers to keep the seas in harmony. Lia was a princess there, but here she was just a strange-looking girl who had to wear a mask to breathe.

She must be missing her dad, he thought. *And do I really feel at home here?*

"I'm not sure," he said at last.

Laughter came from the other room, where Max's parents were catching up, going through old photo albums after so long apart. *This is their place*, Max thought, his fingers touching his gills. *But is it mine?*

Lia suddenly pressed her face right up to the windows, fingers splayed against the glass.

"What's the matter?" said Max.

"I heard something," she said, "from the

sea. Something called my name."

Max couldn't help a smile playing over his lips. "We're 523 storeys up!" he said. "You wouldn't even hear a foghorn from this high."

"I have to go," Lia said, turning and rushing towards the door.

"But we're about to have dinner!" said Max, following her.

"Trust me, Breather-boy. My aqua hearing is better than yours."

She climbed into the lift, followed by Max, and Rivet jumped in beside them. In less than ten seconds, they were at ground level and running towards the docks. Lia leaped up on the harbour wall and into the water with a splash. Max stopped and watched. Sure enough, a pufferfish bobbed in the waves, and beside it, Spike the swordfish rolled in the water. The pufferfish's mouth moved silently, and Lia's brow furrowed.

"It's a message from my father," she called to him. "Something's happened in Sumara… Something bad."

Max felt the air grow chill. "Then we'd better find out what it is."

Lia looked at him, confused. "But…your home is here. You've only just got your mother back."

Max stared up at the skyscraper he called home. He couldn't even see which apartment was theirs from this far below.

Lia's right. There's so much to talk about with my mum. Where's she been all this time? But I can't let Lia swim off into dangerous waters on her own. At least we've stopped Cora and the Professor for now, and I know my parents are safe.

He turned out to sea again. The setting sun left a trail of gold from the horizon to the harbour wall where he stood. Almost like a path, leading to the edge of the ocean.

Max ran along the jetty and found his aquabike. He leaped onto the saddle.

"Rivet come too!" barked his dogbot, wagging his tail.

Lia was taking off her Amphibio mask and clambering onto Spike's back.

"I told you – you don't have to come," she said gently, looking at Max.

Max nodded. *But underwater is where the adventures are. Where my friends are, too.*

"I know that," he said, "but I want to. Here's where my home is – in the sea."

Lia smiled gratefully, then squeezed Spike's side. The swordfish shot off in the blink of an eye. "After them, Riv!" Max said.

The dogbot jumped into the water with a splash. His tail propeller whirred into life.

Max set the aquabike to *DIVE* and ducked

below the waves. Cold water flowed into his gills. It felt natural. And with a twist of the throttle, he lurched through the water in Lia's wake.

Together, they swam down towards unknown dangers.

Don't miss Max's next Sea Quest adventure,
when he faces

REKKAR
THE SCREECHING ORCA

SEA QUEST®

Look out for all the books in
Sea Quest Series 4:

THE LOST LAGOON

REKKAR THE SCREECHING ORCA
TRAGG THE ICE BEAR
HORVOS THE HORROR BIRD
GUBBIX THE POISON FISH

OUT IN SEPTEMBER 2014!

Don't miss the
BRAND NEW
Special Bumper Edition:

978 1 40832 851 4

SKALDA
THE SOUL STEALER

OUT IN JUNE 2014

WIN AN EXCLUSIVE GOODY BAG

In every Sea Quest book the Sea Quest logo is hidden in one of the pictures. Find the logos in books 9-12, make a note of which pages they appear on and go online to enter the competition at

www.seaquestbooks.co.uk

Each month we will put all of the correct entries into a draw and select one winner to receive a special Sea Quest goody bag.

You can also send your entry on a postcard to:

Sea Quest Competition, Orchard Books, 338 Euston Road, London, NW1 3BH

Don't forget to include your name and address!

GOOD LUCK

Closing Date: May 31st 2014

IF YOU LIKE SEA QUEST, YOU'LL LOVE **BEAST QUEST!**

Series 1: COLLECT THEM ALL!

An evil wizard has enchanted the magical beasts of Avantia. Only a true hero can free the beasts and save the land. Is Tom the hero Avantia has been waiting for?

978 1 84616 483 5

978 1 84616 482 8

978 1 84616 484 2

978 1 84616 486 6

978 1 84616 485 9

978 1 84616 487 3